Puppy Mudge Has a Snack

By Cynthia Rylant

Illustrated by Isidre Mones

in the style of Suçie Stevenson

READY-TO-READ

SIMON & SCHUSTER BOOKS FOR YOUNG READERS
New York   London   Toronto   Sydney   Singapore

SIMON & SCHUSTER BOOKS FOR YOUNG READERS
An imprint of Simon & Schuster Children's Publishing Division
1230 Avenue of the Americas, New York, New York 10020

This is Mudge.

He is Henry's puppy.

Mudge wants Henry's snack.

"No, Mudge," says Henry.

Mudge gets on Henry's lap.

"No, Mudge," says Henry.

Mudge wants Henry's snack.

Mudge gets on Henry's head.

"No, Mudge," says Henry.

Mudge wants Henry's snack.

Mudge drools.

"Aw, Mudge," says Henry.

Mudge looks cute.

Mudge looks very, very cute.

Mudge looks too cute.

"Mudge, you are TOO cute,"
says Henry.

Henry gets a snack for Mudge.
It is a CRACKER.

Mudge LOVES crackers.

Now Henry has a snack.
And Mudge has a snack.

And all Mudge had to be was
CUTE!